Sharon N. Delgado

OLD TURTLE'S WINTER GAMES

Written and illustrated by Leonard Kessler

A Young

For snowy days

Published by
Dell Publishing
a division of
Bantam Doubleday Dell Publishing Group, Inc.
666 Fifth Avenue
New York, New York 10103

ISBN: 0-440-40261-1

Reprinted by arrangement with William Morrow & Company, Inc., on
behalf of Greenwillow Books

Printed in the United States of America

January 1990

10   9   8   7   6   5   4   3   2   1

W

CONTENTS

THE SNOW

"Look at that sky,"
    said Old Turtle.
"It looks dark," said Dog.
"Smell the air.
    What does it smell like?"
    Old Turtle asked.
"It smells like air,"
    said Frog.
"No, it smells like snow,"
    said Old Turtle.

5

"Snow is cold.
It makes me shiver,"
said Rabbit.
"I like snow," said Frog.
"Me too," said Duck.
"What can we do
when it snows?"
asked Chicken.

"We can ski," said Owl.

"Skate," said Chicken.

"Go sledding," said Fox.

"Play hockey," said Gull.

"Fall on the ice," said Rabbit.

"We can have winter games,"
said Old Turtle.

"Look," said Chicken.

"It's snowing."

"Yea for snow," Frog cheered.

"Training starts tomorrow
  for the winter games!"
  said Old Turtle.

It snowed all day.
It snowed all night.
In the morning everything
was covered with snow.

"Look at my big tracks
in the white snow," said Duck.
Frog made some snowballs.
POW!
He hit Duck.
POW!
He hit Turtle.

"Now stop that," said Old Turtle.
"No more fooling around.
It's time to get in shape
for the winter games.
We will start with ski jumping,"
he told them.

THE PRACTICE

"Put on your skis," called Duck.
They all slid down the ramp
and jumped.
All but Rabbit.

"I have only one ski.
I can't find the other one,"
he said.
"Oh, Rabbit," said Frog.
"You can't be a ski jumper
with only one ski."

"Skating time,"
called Old Turtle.
Round and round they skated.
"This is how to skate
a figure 8," said Old Turtle.
Rabbit tried to skate.
But he fell down.
"I will help you," said Frog.

"Keep your feet like this.
Bend your knees.
Keep your head up high,
and this is how you stop."

Rabbit tried.
He fell down again.
"Keep trying,"
called Old Turtle.

The next day they learned
how to play ice hockey.
"Whee! This is fun," said Frog.
"Remember," said Old Turtle.
"No tripping. No hitting."

Rabbit tried to play ice hockey.

But he fell down.

"I can't ski. I can't skate.

I can't play hockey.

I can't do anything!" he said.

"Just keep trying," called

Old Turtle. "You will be

in the winter games."

"When do the winter games
begin?" asked Fox.
Turtle smiled.
He put up a big sign.

"I want to win a prize," said Cat.

"Me too," said Fox.

"I never won a prize,"
    said Rabbit.

"You can win a prize
    if you try," Duck told him.

"We will all be trying
    tomorrow," said Gull.

THE GAMES

The next morning
Old Turtle shouted,
"LET THE WINTER
GAMES BEGIN!"

Bluebird blew the horn.

"Line up for the big parade,"

said Old Turtle.

They all marched to the ski ramp.
"Good luck," Old Turtle called
to them.
The jumpers climbed to the top
of the takeoff tower.
It was very quiet.
"Are you scared?" Frog asked Duck.
"I am scared," Duck whispered.
"Me too," whispered Frog.
"But let's jump!" he said.
Duck slid down the ski ramp.
Up in the air she went.
"Good jump," said Turtle.

"It is my turn," said Frog.

WHOOSH!

Down the ramp he went.

Then up, up.

"I'm flying!" he shouted.

"I did it! I did it!"

23

"But you fell when you landed,"
said Duck.
She helped Frog
out of the snow.

The other ski jumpers
went down the ramp
one at a time.

"Owl made the longest jump,"
said Fox.
"Owl set a new record!"

"What's next?" asked Chicken.

"Figure skating," said Turtle.

"Let's put on our skates,"
    said Cat.

"Start the music,"
Old Turtle called.
"Watch us tango,"
said Fox and Chicken.

"Now it is our turn to waltz,"
said Gull and Crow.

"Look at me spin," said Cat.

"I will skate a figure 3,"
said Goose.
"I can skate a figure 8,"
said Raccoon.

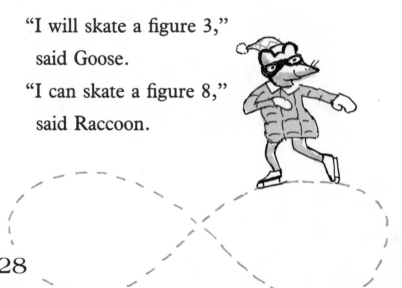

"Oh, I can skate

a bigger number," said Duck.

She skated from here to there.

She skated from there to here.

"What number is that?" asked Frog.

"It's an eleven!" said Duck.

"Ha, ha," she said.

"I am cold," said Rabbit.

"Put on your mittens,"
  said Chicken.

"I need some hot food,"
  said Duck.

"Hot soup," said Frog.

"Hot dogs," said Gull.

  Dog laughed. "Not for me."

"It is getting dark," said Fox.

"Time to go home," said Owl.

"Be here tomorrow

for the big ice hockey game,"

Old Turtle said.

The next day Turtle
announced the lineups.
"Duck, Owl, Cat, Raccoon,
Dog, and Frog are the
BLUE TEAM," he said.
"Gull, Goose, Crow, Fox,
Chicken, and Rabbit are
the GREEN TEAM."
Turtle gave them each
a hockey stick.

"I can't play hockey,"
  said Rabbit, "I am
  just learning how to skate."
"Then Bluebird will play
  for the GREEN TEAM,"
  said Old Turtle.

"Ready for the face-off?"
he asked.
Old Turtle dropped the puck.
"Whee! Let's go, BLUE TEAM!"
shouted Duck.

SWISH!　　　　SLAP SHOT

SNAP SHOT　　　　NO GOAL

NO HITTING   NO FIGHTING

SWISH   GOAL

BLUE TEAM   1

GREEN TEAM   0

35

FACE-OFF **HERE COMES CROW!**

SWISH   SWISH **SLAP SHOT
GOAL!**

BLUE TEAM   1

GREEN TEAM   1

Two minutes to go!

GO, DUCK, GO!

"Game is over. We won!"

yelled the BLUE TEAM. "We won!"

BLUE TEAM 2

GREEN TEAM 1

"What is the next event?"
asked Frog.
"The downhill sled race,"
said Old Turtle.
"I want to be in the race,
but I do not have a sled,"
said Rabbit.

"Oh yes, you do *now*,"
said Turtle.
"Just sit on my shell."

"Everyone line up,"
called Bluebird.
"On your mark.
Get set.
Go!"

Down the hill slid all the racers.

Down the hill went

Turtle and Rabbit.

They passed Duck and Frog.

They passed Goose and Chicken.

"We are coming to a curve.

I can't hold on!" yelled Rabbit.

"Yes, you can!" shouted Turtle.
"Hold on!"

Rabbit held on.

He did not fall.

They passed Owl and Fox.

They passed everybody.

They crossed the finish line.

"Rabbit won!

Rabbit won!" shouted Cat.

"I had the best *sled*,"

said Rabbit.

THE PRIZES

Old Turtle handed out the prizes.

"Everyone won," said Goose.

"Even Rabbit," said Fox.

"But there is *one* more prize,"
   said Duck.

"Start the music,"
   Frog told Bluebird.

"Turtle, please step forward,"
said Duck.
"This prize is for
all of your hard work."

"And for the fastest sled
in the winter games!"
said Rabbit.
"Yea for Old Turtle.
Yea for the winter games,"
they all shouted.

LEONARD KESSLER is a longtime winter sports fan. He is also a great fan of that skilled athlete, fearless and jolly Old Turtle. He is the author-artist of many sports books for young readers: *The Big Mile Race, Old Turtle's Baseball Stories, Super Bowl, Kick, Pass and Run,* and *Here Comes the Strikeout.* Mr. Kessler lives in Rockland County, New York, where he plays his favorite game, tennis, when the snow and ice are gone. He has a little cat who likes snow and ice.